Emile Zola
THE FÊTE AT COQUEVILLE

FRENCH CLASSICS

Emile Zola

THE FÊTE AT COQUEVILLE

(The Coqueville Spree)

Translated by L. G. Meyer

With an essay by Edmund Gosse about
THE SHORT STORIES OF ZOLA

MONDIAL

Mondial
New York

**Emile Zola:
The Fête at Coqueville**
(a.k.a. The Coqueville Spree)

Translated by L. G. Meyer

French original title: "La Fête à Coqueville"

**With an essay about "The Short Stories of Zola"
(ca. 1892) by Edmund Gosse**

Copyright © 2008 Mondial
(for this print edition of
"The Fête at Coqueville")

ISBN 978-1-59569-086-9
Library of Congress Control Number: 2007943728

www.mondialbooks.com

CONTENTS

Edmund Gosse: The Short Stories of Zola

Page I

Emile Zola: The Fête at Coqueville

Page 1

Edmund Gosse

THE SHORT STORIES OF ZOLA

(1892)

THE SHORT STORIES OF ZOLA

It is by his huge novels, and principally by those of the Rougon-Macquart series, that Zola is known to the public and to the critics. Nevertheless, he found time during the forty years of his busy literary career to publish about as many small stories, now comprised in four separate volumes. It is natural that his novels should present so very much wider and more attractive a subject for analysis that, so far as I can discover, even in France no critic has hitherto taken the shorter productions separately, and discussed Zola as a maker of *contes*. Yet there is a very distinct interest in seeing how such a thunderer or bellower on the trumpet can breathe through silver; and, as a matter of fact, the short stories reveal a Zola considerably dissimilar to the author of *Nana* and of *La Terre* — a much more optimistic, romantic, and gentle writer. If, moreover, he had nowhere assailed the decencies more severely than he does in these thirty or forty short stories, he would never have been named among the enemies of Mrs. Grundy, and the gates of the Palais Mazarin would long ago have been opened to receive him. It is, indeed, to a lion with his mane *en papillotes* that I here desire to attract the attention of English readers; to a man-eating monster, indeed, but to one who is on his best behaviour and blinking in the warm sunshine of Provence.

I

The first public appearance of Zola in any form was made as a writer of a short story. A southern journal, *La Provence*, published at Aix, brought out in 1859 a little *conte* entitled *La Fée Amoureuse.* When this was written, in 1858, the future novelist was a student of eighteen, attending the rhetoric classes at the Lycée St. Louis; when it was printed, life in Paris, far from his delicious South, was beginning to open before him, harsh, vague, with a threat of poverty and failure. *La Fée Amoureuse* may still be read by the curious in the *Contes à Ninon*. It is a fantastic little piece, in the taste of the eighteenth-century trifles of Crébillon or Boufflers, written with considerable care in an over-luscious vein—a fairy tale about an enchanted bud of sweet marjoram, which expands and reveals the amorous fay, guardian of the loves of Prince Loïs and the fair Odette. This is a moonlight-coloured piece of un-recognisable Zola, indeed, belonging to the period of his lost essay on "The Blind Milton dictating to his Elder Daughter, while the Younger accompanies him upon the Harp," a piece which many have sighed in vain to see.

He was twenty when, in 1860, during the course of blackening reams of paper with poems à la Musset, he turned, in the aerial garret, or lantern above the garret of 35 Rue St. Victor, to the composition of a second story—*Le Carnet de Danse*. This is addressed to Ninon, the ideal lady of all Zola's early writings—the fleet and jocund virgin of the South, in whom he romantically personifies the Provence after which his whole soul was thirsting in the desert of Paris. This is an exquisite piece of writing—a little too studied, perhaps, too full of opulent and voluptuous adjectives; written, as we may plainly see, under the influence of Théophile Gautier. The story, such as it is, is a conversation between Georgette and the programme-card of her last night's ball. What interest *Le Carnet de Danse* possesses it owes to the style, especially that of the opening pages, in which the joyous Provençal life is elegantly described. The young man, still stumbling in the wrong path, had at least become a writer.

For the next two years Zola was starving, and vainly striving to be a poet. Another "belvedere," as Paul Alexis calls it, another glazed garret above the garret, received him in the Rue Neuve St. Etienne du Mont. Here the squalor of Paris was around him; the young idealist from the forests and lagoons of Provence found himself lost in a loud and horrid world of quarrels, oaths, and dirt, of popping beer-bottles and yelling women. A year, at the age of two-and-twenty, spent in this atmosphere of sordid and noisy vice, left its mark for ever on the spirit of the young observer. He lived on bread and coffee, with two sous' worth of apples upon gala days. He had, on one occasion, even to make an Arab of himself, sitting with the bed-wraps draped about him, because he had pawned his clothes. All the time, serene and ardent, he was writing modern imitations of Dante's *Divina Commedia*, epics on the genesis of the world, didactic hymns to Religion, and love songs by the gross. Towards the close of 1861 this happy misery, this wise folly, came to an end; he obtained a clerkship in the famous publishing house of M. Hachette.

But after these two years of poverty and hardship he began to write a few things which were not in verse. Early in 1862 he again addressed to the visionary Ninon a short story called *Le Sang*. He confesses himself weary, as Ninon also must be, of the coquettings of the rose and the infidelities of the butterfly. He will tell her a terrible tale of real life. But, in fact, he is absolutely in the clouds of the worst romanticism. Four soldiers, round a campfire, suffer agonies of ghostly adventure, in the manner of Hofmann or of Petrus Borel. We seem to have returned to the age of 1830, with its vampires and its ghouls. *Simplice*, which comes next in point of date, is far more characteristic, and here, indeed, we find one talent of the future novelist already developed. Simplice is the son of a worldly king, who despises him for his innocence; the prince slips away into the primeval forest and lives with dragon-flies and water-lilies. In the personal life given to the forest itself, as well as to its inhabitants, we have something very like the future idealisations in *L'Abbé Mouret*, although the touch is yet timid and the flashes of romantic insight fugitive. *Simplice* is an exceedingly pretty fairy story, curiously like what Mrs. Alfred Gatty used to write for sentimental English girls and boys: it was probably inspired to some extent by George Sand.

On a somewhat larger scale is *Les Voleurs et l'Âne*, which belongs to the same period of composition. It is delightful to find Zola describing his garret as "full of flowers and of light, and so high up that sometimes one hears the angels talking on the roof." His story describes a summer day's adventure on the Seine, an improvised picnic of strangers on a grassy island of elms, a siesta disturbed by the somewhat stagey trick of a fantastic coquette. According to his faithful biographer, Paul Alexis, the author, towards the close of 1862, chose another lodging, again a romantic chamber, overlooking this time the whole extent of the cemetery of Montparnasse. In this elegiacal retreat he composed two short stories, *Sœur des Pauvres* and *Celle qui m'aime*. Of these, the former was written as a commission for the young Zola's employer, M. Hachette, who wanted a tale appropriate for a children's newspaper which his firm was publishing. After reading what his clerk submitted to him, the publisher is said to have remarked, "Vous êtes un révolté" and to have returned him the manuscript as "too revolutionary." *Sœur des Pauvres* is a tiresome fable, and it is difficult to understand why Zola has continued to preserve it among his writings. It belongs to the class of semi-realistic stories which Tolstoi has since then composed with such admirable skill. But Zola is not happy among saintly visitants to little holy girls, nor among pieces of gold that turn into bats and rats in the hands of selfish peasants. Why this anodyne little religious fable should ever have been considered revolutionary, it is impossible to conceive.

Of a very different order is *Celle qui m'aime*, a story of real power. Outside a tent, in the suburbs of Paris, a man in a magician's dress stands beating a drum and inviting the passers-by to enter and gaze on the realisation of their dreams, the face of her who loves you. The author is persuaded to go in, and he finds himself in the midst of an assemblage of men and boys, women and girls, who pass up in turn to look through a glass trap in a box. In the description of the various types, as they file by, of the aspect of the interior of the tent, there is the touch of a new hand. The vividness of the study is not maintained; it passes off into romanesque extravagance, but for a few moments the attentive listener, who goes back to these early stories, is conscious that he has heard the genuine accent of the master of Naturalism.

Months passed, and the young Provençal seemed to be making but little progress in the world. His poems definitely failed to find a publisher, and for a while he seems to have flagged even in the production of prose. Towards the beginning of 1864, however, he put together the seven stories which I have already mentioned, added to them a short novel entitled *Aventures du Grand Sidoine*, prefixed a fanciful and very prettily turned address *A Ninon*, and carried off the collection to a new publisher, M. Hetzel. It was accepted, and issued in October of the same year. Zola's first book appeared under the title of *Contes à Ninon*. This volume was very well received by the reviewers, but ten years passed before the growing fame of its author carried it beyond its first edition of one thousand copies.

There is no critical impropriety in considering these early stories, since Zola never allowed them, as he allowed several of his subsequent novels, to pass out of print. Nor, from the point of view of style, is there anything to be ashamed of in them. They are written with an uncertain and an imitative, but always with a careful hand, and some passages of natural description, if a little too precious, are excellently modulated. What is really very curious in the first *Contes à Ninon* is the optimistic tone, the sentimentality, the luscious idealism. The young man takes a cobweb for his canvas, and paints upon it in rainbow-dew with a peacock's feather. Except, for a brief moment, in *Celle qui m'aime*, there is not a phrase that suggests the naturalism of the Rougon-Macquart novels, and it is an amusing circumstance that, while Zola has not only been practising, but very sternly and vivaciously preaching, the gospel of Realism, this innocent volume of fairy stories should all the time have been figuring among his works. The humble student who should turn from the master's criticism to find an example in his writings, and who should fall by chance on the *Contes à Ninon*, would be liable to no small distress of bewilderment.

II

Ten years later, in 1874, Zola published a second volume of short stories, entitled Nouveaux Contes a Ninon. His position, his literary character, had in the meantime undergone a profound modification. In 1874 he was no longer unknown to the public or to himself. He had already published four of the Rougon-Macquart novels, embodying the natural and social history of a French family during the Second Empire. He was scandalous and famous, and already bore a great turbulent name in literature and criticism. The *Nouveaux Contes à Ninon*, composed at intervals during that period of stormy evolution, have the extraordinary interest which attends the incidental work thrown off by a great author during the early and noisy manhood of his talent. After 1864 Zola had written one unsuccessful novel after another, until at last, in *Thérèse Raquin*, with its magnificent study of crime chastised by its own hideous after-gust, he produced a really remarkable performance. The scene in which the paralytic mother tries to denounce the domestic murderers was in itself enough to prove that France possessed one novelist the more.

This was late in 1867, when M. Zola was in his twenty-eighth year. A phrase of Louis Ulbach's, in reviewing *Thérèse Raquin*, which he called "litterature putride," is regarded as having started the question of Naturalism, and M. Zola who had not, up to that time, had any notion of founding a school, or even of moving in any definite direction, was led to adopt the theories which we identify with his name during the angry dispute with

Ulbach. In 1865 he had begun to be drawn towards Edmond and Jules de Goncourt, and to feel, as he puts it, that in the salons of the Parnassians he was growing more and more out of his element "among so many impenitent romantiques." Meanwhile he was for ever feeding the furnaces of journalism, scorched and desiccated by the blaze of public life, by the daily struggle for bread. He was roughly affronting the taste of those who differed from him, with rude hands he was thrusting out of his path the timid, the dull, the old-fashioned. The spectacle of these years of Zola's life is not altogether a pleasant one, but it leaves on us the impression of a colossal purpose pursued with force and courage. In 1871 the first of the Rougon-Macquart novels appeared, and the author was fairly launched on his career. He was writing books of large size, in which he was endeavouring to tell the truth about modern life with absolute veracity, no matter how squalid, or ugly, or venomous that truth might be.

But during the whole of this tempestuous decade Zola, in his hot battlefield of Paris, heard the voice of Ninon calling to him from the leafy hollows, from behind the hawthorn hedges, of his own dewy Provence — the cool Provence of earliest flowery spring. When he caught these accents whistling to his memory from the past, and could no longer resist answering them, he was accustomed to write a little conte, light and innocent, and brief enough to be the note of a caged bird from indoors answering its mate in the trees of the garden. This is the real secret of the utterly incongruous tone of the *Nouveaux Contes* when we compare them with the *Curée* and *Madeleine Férat* of the same period. It would be utterly to misunderstand the nature of Zola to complain, as Pierre Loti did the other day, that the coarseness and cynicism of the naturalistic novel, the tone of a ball at Belleville, could not sincerely co-exist with a love of beauty, or with a nostalgia for youth and country pleasures. In the short stories of the period of which we are speaking, that poet who dies in most middle-aged men lived on for Zola, artificially, in a crystal box carefully addressed "à Ninon là-bas," a box into which, at intervals, the master of the Realists slipped a document of the most refined ideality.

Of these tiny stories there are twelve of them within one hundred pages — not all are quite worthy of his genius. He grimaces a little too much in *Les Epaules de la Marquise*, and M. Bourget has since analysed the little self-indulgent devote of quality more successfully than Zola did in *Le Jeune*. But most of them are very charming. Here is *Le Grand Michu*, a study of gallant, stupid boyhood; here *Les Paradis des Chats*, one of the author's rare escapes into humour. In *Le Forgeron*, with its story of the jaded and cynical town-man, who finds health and happiness by retiring to a lodging within the very thunders of a village blacksmith, we have a profound criticism of life. *Le Petit Village* is interesting to us here, because, with its pathetic picture of *Woerth in Alsace*, it is the earliest of Zola's studies of war. In other of these stories the spirit of Watteau seems to inspire the sooty Vulcan of Naturalism. He prattles of moss-grown fountains, of alleys of wild strawberries, of rendezvous under the wings of the larks, of moonlight strolls in the *bosquets* of a château. In every one, without exception, is absent that tone of brutality which we associate with the notion of Zola's genius. All is gentle irony and pastoral sweetness, or else downright pathetic sentiment.

The volume of Nouveaux *Contes à Ninon* closes with a story which is much longer and considerably more important than the rest. *Les Quatre Journées de*

Jean Gourdon deserves to rank among the very best things to which Zola has signed his name. It is a study of four typical days in the life of a Provençal peasant of the better sort, told by the man himself. In the first of these it is spring: Jean Gourdon is eighteen years of age, and he steals away from the house of his uncle Lazare, a country priest, that he may meet his coy sweetheart Babet by the waters of the broad Durance. His uncle follows and captures him, but the threatened sermon turns into a benediction, the priestly malediction into an impassioned song to the blossoming springtide. Babet and Jean receive the old man's blessing on their betrothal.

Next follows a day in summer, five years later; Jean, as a soldier in the Italian war, goes through the horrors of a battle and is wounded, but not dangerously, in the shoulder. Just as he marches into action he receives a letter from Uncle Lazare and Babet, full of tender fears and tremors; he reads it when he recovers consciousness after the battle. Presently he creeps off to help his excellent colonel, and they support one another till both are carried off to hospital. This episode, which has something in common with the Sevastopol of Tolstoi, is exceedingly ingenious in its observation of the sentiments of a common man under fire.

The third part of the story occurs fifteen years later. Jean and Babet have now long been married, and Uncle Lazare, in extreme old age, has given up his curé, and lives with them in their farm by the river. All things have prospered with them save one. They are rich, healthy, devoted to one another, respected by all their neighbours; but there is a single happiness lacking — they have no child. And now, in the high autumn splendour when the corn and the grapes are ripe, and the lovely Durance winds like a riband of white satin through the gold and purple of the landscape this gift also is to be theirs. A little son is born to them in the midst of the vintage weather, and the old uncle, to whom life has now no further good thing to offer, drops painlessly from life, shaken down like a blown leaf by his excess of joy, on the evening of the birthday of the child.

The optimistic tone has hitherto been so consistently preserved, that we must almost resent the tragedy of the fourth day. This is eighteen years later, and Jean is now an elderly man. His son Jacques is in early manhood. In the midst of their felicity, on a winter's night, the Durance rises in spate, and all are swept away. It is impossible, in a brief sketch, to give an impression of the charm and romantic sweetness of this little masterpiece, a veritable hymn to the Ninon of Provence; but it raises many curious reflections to consider that this exquisitely pathetic pastoral, with all its gracious and tender personages, should have been written by the master of Naturalism, the author of *Germinal* and of *Pot-Bouille*.

III

In 1878, Zola, who had long been wishing for a place whither to escape from the roar of Paris, bought a little property on the right bank of the Seine, between Poissy and Meulan, where he built himself the house which he inhabited to the last, and which he made so famous. Medan, the village in which this property is placed, is a very quiet hamlet of less than two hundred inhabitants, absolutely unillustrious, save that, according to tradition, Charles the Bold was baptized in the font of its parish church. The river lies before it, with its rich meadows, its poplars, its willow groves; a delicious and somnolent air of peace hangs over it, though so close to Paris. Thither the master's particular friends and disciples soon began to gather: that enthusiastic Boswell, Paul Alexis; Guy de Maupassant, a stalwart oarsman, in his skiff, from Rouen; others, whose names were soon to come prominently forward in connection with that naturalistic school of which Zola was the leader.

It was in 1880 that the little hamlet on the Poissy Road awoke to find itself made famous by the publication of a volume which marks an epoch in French literature, and still more in the history of the short story. *Les Soirées de Médan* was a manifesto by the naturalists, the most definite and the most defiant which had up to that time been made. It consisted of six short stories, several of which were of remarkable excellence, and all of which awakened an amount of discussion almost unprecedented. Zola came first with *L'Attaque du Moulin*, which is rather a short novel than a genuine *conte*. The next story was *Boule de Suif*, a veritable masterpiece in a new vein, by an entirely new novelist, a certain M. Guy de Maupassant, thirty years of age, who had been presented to Zola, with warm recommendations, by Gustave Flaubert. The other contributors were M. Henri Céard, who also had as yet published nothing, a man who seems to have greatly impressed all his associates, but who has done little or nothing to justify their hopes; M. Joris-Karl Huysmans, older than the rest, and already somewhat distinguished for picturesque, malodorous novels; M. Léon Hennique, a youth from Guadeloupe, who had attracted attention by a very odd and powerful novel, *La Dévouée*, the story of an inventor who murders his daughter that he may employ her fortune on perfecting his machine; and finally, the faithful Paul Alexis, a native, like Zola himself, of Aix in Provence, and full of the perfervid extravagance of the South. The thread on which the whole book is hung is the supposition that these stories are brought to Médan to be read of an evening to Zola, and that he leads off by telling a tale of his own.

Nothing need be said here, however, of the works of those disciples who placed themselves under the flag of Medan, and little of that story in which, with his accustomed bonhomie of a good giant, Zola accepted their comradeship and consented to march with them. The Attack on the Mill is very well known to English readers, who, even when they have not met with it in the original, have been empowered to estimate its force and truth as a narrative. Whenever Zola writes of war, he writes seriously and well. Like the Julien of his late reminiscences, he has never loved war for its own sake. He has little of the mad and pompous chivalry of the typical Frenchman in his nature. He sees war as the disturber, the annihilator; he recognises in it mainly a destructive, stupid, unintelligible force, set in motion by those in power for the discomfort of ordinary beings, of workers like himself. But in the course of three European wars those of his childhood, of his youth, of his maturity he has come to see beneath the surface, and in *La Débacle* he almost agrees with our young Jacobin poets of one hundred years ago, that Slaughter is God's daughter.

In this connection, and as a commentary on *The Attack on the Mill*, I would commend to the earnest attention of readers the three short papers entitled *Trois Guerres*. Nothing on the subject has been written more picturesque, nor, in its simple way, more poignant, than this triple chain of reminiscences. Whether Louis and Julien existed under those forms, or whether the episodes which they illustrate are fictitious, matters little or nothing. The brothers are natural enough, delightful enough, to belong to the world of fiction, and if their story is, in the historical sense, true, it is one of those rare instances in which fact is better than fancy. The crisis under which the timid Julien, having learned the death of his spirited martial brother, is not broken down, but merely frozen into a cold soldierly passion, and spends the remainder of the campaign— he, the poet, the nestler by the fireside, the timid club-man—in watching behind hedges for Prussians to shoot or stab, is one of the most extraordinary and most interesting that a novelist has ever tried to describe. And the light that it throws on war as a disturber of the moral nature, as a dynamitic force exploding in the midst of an elaborately co-related society, is unsurpassed, even by the studies which Count Lev Tolstoi has made in a similar direction. It is unsurpassed, because it is essentially without prejudice. It admits the discomfort, the horrible vexation and shame of war, and it tears aside the conventional purple and tinsel of it; but at the same time it admits, not without a sigh, that even this clumsy artifice may be the only one available for the cleansing of the people.

IV

In 1883, Zola published a third volume of short stories, under the title of the opening one, *Le Capitaine Burle*. This collection contains the delicate series of brief semi-autobiographical essays called *Aux Champs*, little studies of past impression, touched with a charm which is almost kindred to that of Robert Louis Stevenson's memories. With this exception, the volume consists of four short stories, and of a set of little death-bed anecdotes, called *Comment on Meurt*. This latter is hardly in the writer's best style, and suffers by suggesting the immeasurably finer and deeper studies of the same kind which the genius of Tolstoi has elaborated. Of these little sketches of death, one alone, that of Madame Rousseau, the stationer's wife, is quite of the best class. This is an excellent episode from the sort of Parisian life which Zola understands best, the lower middle class, the small and active shopkeeper, who just contrives to be respectable and no more. The others seem to be invented rather than observed.

The four stories which make up the bulk of this book are almost typical examples of Zola's mature style. They are worked out with extreme care, they display in every turn the skill of the practised narrator, they are solid and yet buoyant in style, and the construction of each may be said to be faultless. It is faultless to a fault; in other words, the error of the author is to be mechanically and inevitably correct. It is difficult to define wherein the over-elaboration shows itself, but in every case the close of the story leaves us sceptical and cold. The denouement is too brilliant and conclusive, the threads are drawn together with too much evidence of preoccupation. The impression is not so much of a true tale told as of an extraordinary situation frigidly written up to and accounted for. In each case a certain social condition is described at the beginning, and a totally opposite condition is discovered at the end of the story. We are tempted to believe that the author determined to do this, to turn the whole box of bricks absolutely topsy-turvy. This disregard of the soft and supple contours of nature, this rugged air of molten metal, takes away from the pleasure we should otherwise legitimately receive from the exhibition of so much fancy, so much knowledge, so many proofs of observation.

The story which gives its name to the book, *Le Capitaine Burle*, is perhaps the best, because it has least of this air of artifice. In a military county town, a captain, who lives with his anxious mother and his little pallid, motherless son, sinks into vicious excesses, and pilfers from the regiment to pay for his vices. It is a great object with the excellent major, who discovers this condition, to save his friend the captain in some way which will prevent an open scandal, and leave the child free for ultimate success in the army. After trying every method, and discovering that the moral nature of the captain is altogether too soft and too far sunken to be redeemed, as the inevitable hour of publicity approaches, the major insults his friend in a café, so as to give him an opportunity of fighting a duel and dying honourably. This is done, and the scandal is evaded, without, however, any good being thereby secured to the family, for the little boy dies of weakness and his grandmother starves. Still, the name of Burle has not been dragged through the mud.

Zola has rarely displayed the quality of humour, but it is present in the story called *La Fête à Coqueville*. Coqueville is the name given to a very remote Norman fishing-village, set in a gorge of rocks, and almost inaccessible except from the sea. Here a sturdy population of some hundred and eighty souls, all sprung from one or other of two rival families, live in the condition of a tiny Verona, torn between contending interests. A ship laden with liqueurs is wrecked on the rocks outside, and one precious cask after another comes riding into Coqueville over the breakers. The villagers, to whom brandy itself has hitherto been the rarest of luxuries, spend a glorious week of perfumed inebriety, sucking splinters that drip with bénedictine, catching noyau in iron cups, and supping up curaçao from the bottom of a boat. Upon this happy shore chartreuse flows like cider, and trappistine is drunk out of a mug. The rarest drinks of the world — Chios mastic and Servian sliwowitz, Jamaica rum and arrack, crême de moka and raki — drip among the mackerel nets and deluge the seaweed. In the presence of this extraordinary and fantastic bacchanal all the disputes of the rival families are forgotten, class prejudices are drowned, and the mayor's rich daughter marries the poorest of the fisher-sons of the enemy's camp. It is very amusingly and very picturesquely told, but spoiled a little by Zola's pet sin — the overcrowding of details, the theatrical completeness and orchestral big-drum of the final scene. Too many barrels of liqueur come in, the village becomes too universally drunk, the scene at last becomes too Lydian for credence.

In the two remaining stories of this collection *Pour une Nuit d' Amour* and *L'Inondation* the fault of mechanical construction is still more plainly obvious. Each of these narratives begins with a carefully accentuated picture of a serene life: in the first instance, that of a timid lad sequestered in a country town; in the second, that of a prosperous farmer, surrounded by his family and enjoying all the delights of material and moral success. In each case this serenity is but the prelude to events of the most appalling tragedy — a tragedy which does not merely strike or wound, but positively annihilates. The story called *L'Inondation*, which describes the results of a bore on the Garonne, would be as pathetic as it is enthralling, exciting, and effective, if the destruction were not so absolutely complete, if the persons so carefully enumerated at the opening of the piece were not all of them sacrificed, and, as in the once popular song called *"An 'Orrible Tale,"* each by some different death of peculiar ingenuity. As to *Pour une Nuit d Amour*, it is not needful to do more than say that it is one of the most repulsive productions ever published by its author, and a vivid exception to the general innocuous character of his short stories.

No little interest, to the practical student of literature, attaches to the fact that in *L'Inondation* Zola is really re-writing, in a more elaborate form, the fourth section of his *Jean Gourdon*. Here, as there, a farmer who has lived in the greatest prosperity, close to a great river, is stripped of everything — of his house, his wealth, and his family — by a sudden rising of the waters. It is unusual for an author thus to re-edit a work, or tell the same tale a second time at fuller length, but the sequences of incidents will be found to be closely identical, although the later is by far the larger and the more populous story. It is not uninteresting to the technical student to compare the two pieces, the composition of which was separated by about ten years.

V

Finally, in 1884, Zola published a fourth collection, named, after the first of the series, *Naïs Micoulin*. This volume contained in all six stories, each of considerable extent. I do not propose to dwell at any length on the contents of this book, partly because they belong to the finished period of naturalism, and seem more like castaway fragments of the Rougon-Macquart epos than like independent creations, but also because they clash with the picture I have sought to draw of an optimistic and romantic Zola returning from time to time to the short story as a shelter from his theories. Of these tales, one or two are trifling and passably insipid; the Parisian sketches called *Nantas* and *Madame Neigon* have little to be said in favour of their existence. Here Zola seems desirous to prove to us that he could write as good Octave Feuillet, if he chose, as the author of *Monsieur de Cantors* himself. In *Les Coquillages de M. Chabre*, which I confess I read when it first appeared, and have now re-read with amusement, we see the heavy Zola endeavouring to sport as gracefully as M. de Maupassant, and in the same style. The impression of buoyant Atlantic seas and hollow caverns is well rendered in this most unedifying story. *Naïs Micoulin*, which gives its name to the book, is a disagreeable tale of seduction and revenge in Provence, narrated with the usual ponderous conscientiousness. In each of the last mentioned the background of landscape is so vivid that we half forgive the faults of the narrative.

The two remaining stories in the book are more remarkable, and one of them, at least, is of positive value. It is curious that in *La Mort d'Olivier Bécailles* and *Jacques Damour* Zola should in the same volume present versions of the *Enoch Arden* story, the now familiar episode of the man who is supposed to be dead, and comes back to find his wife re-married. Olivier Bécaille is a poor clerk, lately arrived in Paris with his wife; he is in wretched health, and has always been subject to cataleptic seizures. In one of these he falls into a state of syncope so prolonged that they believe him to be dead, and bury him. He manages to break out of his coffin in the cemetery, and is picked up fainting by a philanthropic doctor. He has a long illness, at the end of which he cannot discover what has become of his wife. After a long search, he finds that she has married a very excellent young fellow, a neighbour; and in the face of her happiness, Olivier Bécaille has not the courage to disturb her. Like Tennyson's "strong, heroic soul," he passes out into the silence and the darkness.

The exceedingly powerful story called *Jacques Damour* treats the same idea, but with far greater mastery, and in a less conventional manner.

Jacques Damour is a Parisian artisan, who becomes demoralised during the *siège*, and joins the Commune. He is captured by the Versailles army, and sentenced to penal servitude in New Caledonia, leaving a wife and a little girl behind him in Paris. After some years, in company with two or three other convicts, he makes an attempt to escape. He, in fact, succeeds in escaping, with one companion, the rest being drowned before they get out of the colony. One of the dead men being mistaken for him, Jacques Damour is reported home deceased. When, after credible adventures, and at the declaration of the amnesty, he returns to Paris, his wife and daughter have disappeared. At length he finds the former married to a prosperous butcher in the Batignolles, and he summons up courage, egged on by a rascally friend, to go to the shop in midday and claim his lawful wife. The successive scenes in the shop, and the final one, in which the ruddy butcher, sure of his advantage over this squalid and prematurely wasted ex-convict, bids Félicie take her choice, are superb. Zola has done nothing more forcible or life-like. The poor old Damour retires, but he still has a daughter to discover. The finale of the tale is excessively unfitted for the young person, and no serious critic could do otherwise than blame it. But, at the same time, I am hardened enough to admit that I think it very true to life and not a little humorous, which, I hope, is not equivalent to a moral commendation. We may, if we like, wish that Zola had never written *Jacques Damour*, but nothing can prevent it from being a superbly constructed and supported piece of narrative, marred by unusually few of the mechanical faults of his later work.

The consideration of the optimistic and sometimes even sentimental short stories of Zola helps to reveal to a candid reader the undercurrent of pity which exists even in the most "naturalistic" of his romances. It cannot be too often insisted upon that, although he tried to write books as scientific as anything by Pasteur or Claude Bernard, he simply could not do it. His innate romanticism would break through, and, for all his efforts, it made itself apparent even when he strove with the greatest violence to conceal it. In his conies he does not try to fight against his native idealism, and they are, in consequence, perhaps the most genuinely characteristic productions of his pen which exist.

Emile Zola

THE FÊTE AT COQUEVILLE

I

Coqueville is a little village planted in a cleft in the rocks, two leagues from Grandport. A fine sandy beach stretches in front of the huts lodged half-way up in the side of the cliff like shells left there by the tide. As one climbs to the heights of Grandport, on the left the yellow sheet of sand can be very clearly seen to the west like a river of gold dust streaming from the gaping cleft in the rock; and with good eyes one can even distinguish the houses, whose tones of rust spot the rock and whose chimneys send up their bluish trails to the very crest of the great slope, streaking the sky. It is a deserted hole. Coqueville has never been able to attain to the figure of two hundred inhabitants. The gorge which opens into the sea, and on the threshold of which the village is planted, burrows into the earth by turns so abrupt and by descents so steep that it is almost impossible to pass there with wagons. It cuts off all communication and isolates the country so that one seems to be a hundred leagues from the neighboring hamlets. Moreover, the inhabitants have communication with Grandport only by water. Nearly all of them fishermen, living by the ocean, they carry their fish there every day in their barks. A great commission house, the firm of Dufeu, buys their fish on contract. The father Dufeu has been dead some years, but the widow Dufeu has continued the business; she has simply engaged a clerk, M. Mouchel, a big blond devil, charged with beating up the coast and dealing with the fishermen. This M. Mouchel is the sole link between Coqueville and the civilized world.

Coqueville merits a historian. It seems certain that the village, in the night of time, was founded by the Mahés; a family which happened to establish itself there and which grew vigorous at the foot of the cliff. These Mahés continued to prosper at first, marrying continually among themselves, for during centuries one finds none but Mahés there. Then under Louis XIII appeared one Floche. No one knew too much of where he came from. He married a Mahé, and from that time a phenomenon was brought forth; the Floches in their turn prospered and multiplied exceedingly, so that they ended little by little in absorbing the Mahés whose numbers diminished until their fortune passed entirely into the hands of the newcomers. Without doubt, the Floches brought new blood, more vigorous physical organs, a temperament which adapted itself better to that hard condition of high wind and of high sea. At any rate, they are to-day masters of Coqueville.

It can easily be understood that this displacement of numbers and of riches was not accomplished without terrible disturbances. The Mahés and the Floches detest each other. Between them is a hatred of centuries. The Mahés in spite of their decline retain the pride of ancient conquerors. After all they are the founders, the ancestors. They speak with contempt of the first Floche, a beggar, a vagabond picked up by them from feelings of pity, and to have given away one of their daughters to whom was their eternal regret. This Floche, to hear them speak, had engendered nothing but a descent of libertines and thieves, who pass their nights in raising children and their days in coveting legacies. And there is not an insult they do not heap upon the powerful tribe of Floche, seized with that bitter rage of nobles, decimated, ruined, who see the spawn of the bourgeoisie master of their rents and of their châteaux. The Floches, on their side, naturally have the insolence of those who triumph. They are in full possession, a thing to make them insolent. Full of contempt for the ancient race of the Mahés, they threaten to drive them from the village if they do not bow their heads. To them they are starvelings, who instead of draping themselves in their rags would do much better to mend them.

So Coqueville finds itself a prey to two fierce factions—something like one hundred and thirty inhabitants bent upon devouring the other fifty for the simple reason that they are the stronger.

The struggle between two great empires has no other history.

Among the quarrels which have lately upset Coqueville, they cite the famous enmity of the brothers, Fouasse and Tupain, and the ringing battles of the Rouget menage. You must know that every inhabitant in former days received a surname, which has become to-day the regular name of the family; for it was difficult to distinguish one's self among the cross-breedings of the Mahés and the Floches. Rouget assuredly had an ancestor of fiery blood. As for Fouasse and Tupain, they were called thus without knowing why, many surnames having lost all rational meaning in course of time. Well, old Franchise, a wanton of eighty years who lived forever, had had Fouasse by a Mahé, then becoming a widow, she remarried with a Floche and brought forth Tupain. Hence the hatred of the two brothers, made specially lively by the question of inheritance. At the Rouget's they beat each other to a jelly because Rouget accused his wife, Marie, of being unfaithful to him for a Floche, the tall Brisemotte, a strong, dark man, on whom he had already twice thrown himself with a knife, yelling that he would rip open his belly. Rouget, a small, nervous man, was a great spitfire.

But that which interested Coqueville most deeply was neither the tantrums of Rouget nor the differences between Tupain and Fouasse. A great rumor circulated: Delphin, a Mahé, a rascal of twenty years, dared to love the beautiful Margot, the daughter of La Queue, the richest of the Floches and chief man of the country. This La Queue was, in truth, a considerable personage. They called him La Queue because his father, in the days of Louis Philippe, had been the last to tie up his hair, with the obstinacy of old age that clings to the fashions of its youth. Well, then, La Queue owned one of the two large fishing smacks of Coqueville, the "Zephir," by far the best, still quite new and seaworthy. The other big boat, the "Baleine," a rotten old patache*, belonged to Rouget, whose sailors were Delphin and Fouasse, while La Queue took with him Tupain and Brisemotte. These last had grown weary of laughing contemptuously at the "Baleine"; a sabot, they said, which would disappear some fine day under the billows like a handful of mud. So when La Queue learned that that ragamuffin of a Delphin, the froth of the "Baleine," allowed himself to go prowling around his daughter, he delivered two sound whacks at Margot, a trifle merely to warn her that she should never be the wife of a Mahé. As a result, Margot, furious, declared that she would pass that pair of slaps on

---

* Naval term signifying a rickety old concern.

to Delphin if he ever ventured to rub against her skirts. It was vexing to be boxed on the ears for a boy whom she had never looked in the face!

Margot, at sixteen years strong as a man and handsome as a lady, had the reputation of being a scornful person, very hard on lovers. And from that, added to the trifle of the two slaps, of the presumptuousness of Delphin, and of the wrath of Margot, one ought easily to comprehend the endless gossip of Coqueville.

Notwithstanding, certain persons said that Margot, at bottom, was not so very furious at sight of Delphin circling around her. This Delphin was a little blonde, with skin bronzed by the sea-glare, and with a mane of curly hair that fell over his eyes and in his neck. And very powerful despite his slight figure; quite capable of thrashing any one three times his size. They said that at times he ran away and passed the night in Grandport. That gave him the reputation of a werwolf with the girls, who accused him, among themselves, of "making a life of it" — a vague expression in which they included all sorts of unknown pleasures. Margot, when she spoke of Delphin, betrayed too much feeling. He, smiling with an artful air, looked at her with eyes half shut and glittering, without troubling himself the least in the world over her scorn or her transports of passion. He passed before her door, he glided along by the bushes watching for her hours at a time, full of the patience and the cunning of a cat lying in wait for a tomtit; and when suddenly she discovered him behind her skirts, so close to her at times that she guessed it by the warmth of his breath, he did not fly, he took on an air gentle and melancholy which left her abashed, stifled, not regaining her wrath until he was some distance away. Surely, if her father saw her he would smite her again. But she boasted in vain that Delphin would some day get that pair of slaps she had promised him; she never seized the moment to apply them when he was there; which made people say that she ought not to talk so much, since in the end she kept the slaps herself.

No one, however, supposed she could ever be Delphin's wife. In her case they saw the weakness of a coquette. As for a marriage between the most beggarly of the Mahés, a fellow who had not six shirts to set up housekeeping with, and the daughter of the mayor, the richest heiress of the Floches, it would seem simply monstrous. Evil tongues insinuated that she could perfectly go with him all the same, but that she would certainly not marry him. A rich girl takes her pleasure as it suits her, only if she has a head, she does not commit a folly. Finally all Coqueville interested itself in the matter, curious to know how things would turn out. Would Delphin get his two slaps? or else Margot, would she let herself be kissed on both cheeks in some hole in the cliff? They must see! There were some for the slaps and there were some for the kisses. Coqueville was in revolution.

In the village two people only, the curé and the *garde champêtre** belonged neither to the Mahés nor to the Floches. The *garde champêtre*, a tall, dried-up fellow, whose name no one knew, but who was called the Emperor, no doubt because he had served under Charles X, as a matter of fact exercised no burdensome supervision over the commune which was all bare rocks and waste lands. A sub-prefect who patronized him had created for him the sinecure where he devoured in peace his very small living.

As for the Abbé Radiguet, he was one of those simple-minded priests whom the bishop, in his de-

---

* Watchman.

sire to be rid of him, buries in some out of the way hole. He lived the life of an honest man, once more turned peasant, hoeing his little garden redeemed from the rock, smoking his pipe and watching his salads grow. His sole fault was a gluttony which he knew not how to refine, reduced to adoring mackerel and to drinking, at times, more cider than he could contain. In other respects, the father of his parishioners, who came at long intervals to hear a mass to please him.

But the curé and the *garde champêtre* were obliged to take sides after having succeeded for a long time in remaining neutral. Now, the Emperor held for the Mahés, while the Abbé Radiguet supported the Floches. Hence complications. As the Emperor, from morning to night, lived like a bourgeois citizen, and, as he wearied of counting the boats which put out from Grandport, he took it upon himself to act as village police. Having become the partizan of the Mahés, through native instinct for the preservation of society, he sided with Fouasse against Tupain; he tried to catch the wife of Rouget in flagrante delicto with Brisemotte, and above all he closed his eyes when he saw Delphin slipping into Margot's courtyard. The worst of it was that these tactics brought about heated quarrels between the Emperor and his natural superior, the mayor La Queue. Respectful of discipline, the former heard the reproaches of the latter, then recommenced to act as his head dictated; which disorganized the public authority of Coqueville. One could not pass before the shed ornamented with the name of the town hall without being deafened by the noise of some dispute. On the other hand, the Abbé Radiguet rallied to the triumphant Floches, who loaded him with superb mackerel, secretly encouraged the resistance of Rouget's wife and threatened Margot with the flames of hell if she should ever allow Delphin to touch her with his finger. It was, to sum up, complete anarchy; the army in revolt against the civil power, religion making itself complaisant toward the pleasures of the bourgoisie; a whole people, a hundred and eighty inhabitants, devouring each other in a hole, in face of the vast sea, and of the infinite sky.

Alone, in the midst of topsy-turvy Coqueville, Delphin preserved the laughter of a love-sick boy, who scorned the rest, provided Margot was for him. He followed her zigzags as one follows hares. Very wise, despite his simple look, he wanted the curé to marry them, so that his bliss might last forever.

One evening, in a byway where he was watching for her, Margot at last raised her hand. But she stopped, all red; for without waiting for the slap, he had seized the hand that threatened him and kissed it furiously. As she trembled, he said to her in a low voice: "I love you. Won't you have me?"

"Never!" she cried, in rebellion.

He shrugged his shoulders, then with an air, calm and tender, "Pray do not say that we shall be very comfortable together, we two. You will see how nice it is."

II

That Sunday the weather was appalling, one of those sudden calamities of September that unchain such fearful tempests on the rocky coast of Grandport. At nightfall Coqueville sighted a ship in distress driven by the wind. But the shadows deepened, they could not dream of rendering help. Since the evening before, the "Zephir" and the "Baleine" had been moored in the little natural harbor situated at the left of the beach, between two walls of granite. Neither La Queue nor Rouget had dared to go out. The worst of it was that M. Mouchel, representing the Widow Dufeu, had taken the trouble to come in person that Saturday to promise them a reward if they would make a serious effort; fish was scarce, they were complaining at the markets. So, Sunday evening, going to bed under squalls of rain, Coqueville growled in a bad humor. It was the everlasting story: orders kept coming in while the sea guarded its fish. And all the village talked of the ship which they had seen passing in the hurricane, and which must assuredly by that time be sleeping at the bottom of the water. The next day, Monday, the sky was dark as ever. The sea, still high, raged without being able to calm itself, although the wind was blowing less strong. It fell completely, but the waves kept up their furious motion. In spite of everything, the two boats went out in the afternoon. Toward four o'clock, the "Zephir" came in again, having caught nothing. While the sailors, Tupain and Brisemotte, anchored in the little harbor, La Queue, exasperated, on the shore, shook his fist at the ocean. And M. Mouchel was waiting! Margot was there, with the half of Coqueville, watching the last surgings of the tempest, sharing her father's rancor against the sea and the sky.

"But where is the 'Baleine'?" demanded some one.

THE FÊTE AT COQUEVILLE

"Out there beyond the point," said La Queue. "If that carcass comes back whole to-day, it will be by a chance."

He was full of contempt. Then he informed them that it was good for the Mahés to risk their skins in that way; when one is not worth a sou, one may perish. As for him, he preferred to break his word to M. Mouchel.

In the mean time, Margot was examining the point of rocks behind which the "Baleine" was hidden.

"Father," she asked at last, "have they caught something?"

"They?" he cried. "Nothing at all."

He calmed himself and added more gently, seeing the Emperor, who was sneering at him:

"I do not know whether they have caught anything, but as they never do catch anything"

"Perhaps, to-day, all the same, they have taken something," said the Emperor ill-naturedly. "Such things have been seen." La Queue was about to reply angrily. But the Abbé Radiguet, who came up, calmed him. From the porch of the church the

Abbé had happened to observe the "Baleine"; and the bark seemed to be giving chase to some big fish. This news greatly interested Coqueville. In the groups reunited on the shore there were Mahés and Floches, the former praying that the boat might come in with a miraculous catch, the others making vows that it might come in empty.

Margot, holding herself very straight, did not take her eyes from the sea. "There they are!" said she simply.

And in fact a black dot showed itself beyond the point. All looked at it. One would have said a cork dancing on the water. The Emperor did not see even the black dot. One must be of Coqueville to recognize at that distance the "Baleine" and those who manned her.

"See!" said Margot, who had the best eyes of the coast, "it is Fouasse and Rouget who are rowing The little one is standing up in the bow."

She called Delphin "the little one" so as not to mention his name. And from then on they followed the course of the bark, trying to account for her strange movements. As the curé said, she appeared to be giving chase to some great fish that might be fleeing before her. That seemed extraordinary. The Emperor pretended that their net was without doubt being carried away. But La Queue cried that they were do-nothings, and that they were just amusing themselves. Quite certain they were not fishing for seals! All the Floches made merry over that joke; while the Mahés, vexed, declared that Rouget was a fine fellow all the same, and that he was risking his skin while others at the least puff of wind preferred terra firma. The Abbé Radiguet was forced to interpose again for there were slaps in the air.

"What ails them?" said Margot abruptly. "They are off again!" They ceased menacing one another, and every eye searched the horizon. The "Baleine" was once more hidden behind the point. This time La Queue himself became uneasy. He could not account for such maneuvres. The fear that Rouget was really in a fair way to catch some fish threw him off his mental balance. No one left the beach, although there was nothing strange to be seen. They stayed there nearly two hours, they watched incessantly for the bark, which appeared from time to time, then disappeared. It finished by not showing itself at all any more. La Queue, enraged, breathing in his heart the abominable wish, declared that she must have sunk; and, as just at that moment Rouget's wife appeared with Brisemotte, he looked at them both, sneering, while he patted Tupain on the shoulder to console him already for the death of his brother, Fouasse. But he stopped laughing when he caught sight of his daughter Margot, silent and looming, her eyes on the distance; it was quite possibly for Delphin.

"What are you up to over there?" he scolded. "Be off home with you! Mind, Margot!"

She did not stir. Then all at once: "Ah! there they are!"

He gave a cry of surprise. Margot, with her good eyes, swore that she no longer saw a soul in the bark; neither Rouget, nor Fouasse, nor any one! The "Baleine," as if abandoned, ran before the wind, tacking about every minute, rocking herself with a lazy air.

A west wind had fortunately risen and was driving her toward the land, but with strange caprices which tossed her to right and to left. Then all Coqueville ran down to the shore. One half shouted to the other half, there remained not a girl in the houses to look after the soup. It was a catastrophe; something inexplicable, the strangeness of which completely turned their heads. Marie, the wife of Rouget, after a moment's reflection, thought it her duty to burst into tears. Tupain succeeded in merely carrying an air of affliction. All the Mahés were in great distress, while the Floches tried to appear conventional. Margot collapsed as if she had her legs broken.

"What are you up to again!" cried La Queue, who stumbled upon her.

"I am tired," she answered simply.

And she turned her face toward the sea, her cheeks between her hands, shading her eyes with the ends of her fingers, gazing fixedly at the bark rocking itself idly on the waves with the air of a good fellow who has drunk too much.

In the mean while suppositions were rife. Perhaps the three men had fallen into the water? Only, all three at a time, that seemed absurd. La Queue would have liked well to persuade them that the "Baleine" had gone to pieces like a rotten egg; but the boat still held the sea; they shrugged their shoulders. Then, as if the three men had actually perished, he remembered that he was Mayor and spoke of formalities.

"Leave off!" cried the Emperor, "Does one die in such a silly way?"

"If they had fallen overboard, little Delphin would have been here by this!"

All Coqueville had to agree, Delphin swam like a herring. But where then could the three men be? They shouted: "I tell you, yes!" "I tell you, no!" "Too stupid!" "Stupid yourself!" And matters came to the point of exchanging blows. The Abbé Radiguet was obliged to make an appeal for reconciliation, while the Emperor hustled the crowd about to establish order. Meanwhile, the bark, without haste, continued to dance before the world. It waltzed, seeming to mock at the people; the sea carried her in, making her salute the land in long rhythmic reverences. Surely it was a bark in a crazy fit. Margot, her cheeks between her hands, kept always gazing. A yawl had just put out of the harbor to go to meet the "Baleine." It was Brisemotte, who had exhibited that impatience, as if he had been delayed in giving certainty to Rouget's wife. From that moment all Coqueville interested itself in the yawl. The voices rose higher: "Well, does he see anything?" The "Baleine" advanced with her mysterious and mocking air. At last they saw him draw himself up and look into the bark that he had succeeded in taking in tow. All held their breath. But, abruptly, he burst out laughing. That was a surprise; what had he to be amused at? "What is it? What have you got there?" they shouted to him furiously.

He, without replying, laughed still louder. He made gestures as if to say that they would see. Then having fastened the "Baleine" to the yawl, he towed her back. And an unlooked-for spectacle stunned Coqueville. In the bottom of the bark, the three men Rouget, Delphin, Fouasse were beatifically stretched out on their backs, snoring, with fists clenched, dead drunk. In their midst was found a little cask stove in, some full cask they had come across at sea and which they had appreciated. Without doubt, it was very good, for they had drunk it all save a liter's worth which had leaked into the bark and which was mixed with the sea water.

"Ah! the pig!" cried the wife of Rouget, brutally, ceasing to whimper.

"Well, it's characteristic their catch!" said La Queue, who affected great disgust.

"Forsooth!" replied the Emperor, "they catch what they can! They have at least caught a cask, while others have not caught anything at all."

The Mayor shut up, greatly vexed. Coqueville brayed. They understood now. When barks are intoxicated, they dance as men do; and that one, in truth, had her belly full of liquor. Ah, the slut! What a minx! She festooned over the ocean with the air of a sot who could no longer recognize his home. And Coqueville laughed, and fumed, the Mahés found it funny, while the Floches found it disgusting. They surrounded the "Baleine," they craned their necks, they strained their eyes to see sleeping there the three jolly dogs who were exposing the secret springs of their jubilation, oblivious of the crowd hanging over them. The abuse and the laughter troubled them but little. Rouget did not hear his wife accuse him of drinking up all they had; Fouasse did not feel the stealthy kicks with which his brother Tupain rammed his sides. As for Delphin, he was pretty, after he had drunk, with his blond hair, his rosy face drowned in bliss. Margot had gotten up, and silently, for the present, she contemplated the little fellow with a hard expression.

"Must put them to bed!" cried a voice.

But just then Delphin opened his eyes. He rolled looks of rapture over the people. They questioned him on all sides with an eagerness that dazed him somewhat, the more easily since he was still as drunk as a thrush.

"Well! What?" he stuttered; "it was a little cas — There is no fish. Therefore, we have caught a little cask."

He did not get beyond that. To every sentence he added simply: "It was very good!"

"But what was it in the cask?" they asked him hotly.

"Ah! I don't know — it was very good."

By this time Coqueville was burning to know. Every one lowered their noses to the boat, sniffing vigorously. With one opinion, it smelt of liquor; only no one could guess what liquor. The Emperor, who flattered himself that he had drunk of everything that a man can drink, said that he would see. He solemnly took in the palm of his hand a little of the liquor that was swimming in the bottom of the bark. The crowd became all at once silent. They waited. But the Emperor, after sucking up a mouthful, shook his head as if still badly informed. He sucked twice, more and more embarrassed, with an air of uneasiness and surprise. And he was bound to confess:

"I do not know — It's strange — If there was no salt water in it, I would know, no doubt — My word of honor, it is very strange!"

They looked at him. They stood struck with awe before that which the Emperor himself did not venture to pronounce. Coqueville contemplated with respect the little empty cask.

"It was very good!" once more said Delphin, who seemed to be making game of the people. Then, indicating the sea with a comprehensive sweep, he added: "If you want some, there is more there — I saw them little casks little casks little casks"

And he rocked himself with the refrain which he kept singing, gazing tenderly at Margot. He had just caught sight of her. Furious, she made a motion as if to slap him; but he did not even close his eyes; he awaited the slap with an air of tenderness.

The Abbé Radiguet, puzzled by that unknown tipple, he, too, dipped his finger in the bark and sucked it. Like the Emperor, he shook his head: no, he was not familiar with that, it was very extraordinary. They agreed on but one point: the cask must have been wreckage from the ship in distress, signaled Sunday evening. The English ships often carried to Grandport such cargoes of liquor and fine wines.

Little by little the day faded and the people were withdrawn into shadow. But La Queue remained absorbed, tormented by an idea which he no longer expressed. He stopped, he listened a last time to Delphin, whom they were carrying along, and who was repeating in his sing-song voice: "Little casks little casks little casks if you want some, there are more!"

III

That night the weather changed completely. When Coqueville awoke the following day an unclouded sun was shining; the sea spread out without a wrinkle, like a great piece of green satin. And it was warm, one of those pale glows of autumn.

First of the village, La Queue had risen, still clouded from the dreams of the night. He kept looking for a long time toward the sea, to the right, to the left. At last, with a sour look, he said that he must in any event satisfy M. Mouchel. And he went away at once with Tupain and Brisemotte, threatening Margot to touch up her sides if she did not walk straight. As the "Zephir" left the harbor, and as he saw the "Baleine" swinging heavily at her anchor, he cheered up a little, saying: "To-day, I guess, not a bit of it! Blow out the candle, Jeanetton! those gentlemen have gone to bed!"

And as soon as the "Zephir" had reached the open sea, La Queue cast his nets. After that he went to visit his "jambins." The jambins are a kind of elongated eel-pot in which they catch more, especially lobsters and red gurnet. But in spite of the calm sea, he did well to visit his jambins one by one. All were empty; at the bottom of the last one, as if in mockery, he found a little mackerel, which he threw back angrily into the sea. It was fate; there were weeks like that when the fish flouted Coqueville, and always at a time when M. Mouchel had expressed a particular desire for them. When La Queue drew in his nets, an hour later, he found nothing but a bunch of seaweed. Straightway he swore, his fists clenched, raging so much the more for the vast serenity of the ocean, lazy and sleeping like a sheet of burnished silver under the blue sky. The "Zephir," without a waver, glided along in gentle ease. La Queue decided to go in again, after having cast his nets once more. In the afternoon he came to see them, and he menaced God and the saints, cursing in abominable words.

In the mean while, Rouget, Fouasse, and Delphin kept on sleeping. They did not succeed in standing up until the dinner hour. They recollected nothing, they were conscious only of having been treated to something extraordinary, something which they did not understand. In the afternoon, as they were all three down at the harbor, the Emperor tried to question them concerning the liquor, now that they had recovered their senses. It was like, perhaps, eau-de-vie with liquorice-juice in it; or rather one might say rum, sugared and burned. They said "Yes"; they said "No." From their replies, the Emperor suspected that it was ratafia; but he would not have sworn to it. That day Rouget and his men had too many pains in their sides to go a-fishing. Moreover, they knew that La Queue had gone out without success that morning, and they talked of waiting until the next day before visiting their jambins. All three of them, seated on blocks of stone, watched the tide come in, their backs rounded, their mouths clammy, half-asleep.

But suddenly Delphin woke up; he jumped on to the stone, his eyes on the distance, crying: "Look, Boss, off there!"

"What?" asked Rouget, who stretched his limbs.

"A cask."

Rouget and Fouasse were at once on their feet, their eyes gleaming, sweeping the horizon.

"Where is it, lad? Where is the cask?" repeated the boss, greatly moved.

"Off there to the left that black spot."

The others saw nothing. Then Rouget swore an oath. "Nom de Dieu!"

He had just spotted the cask, big as a lentil on the white water in a slanting ray of the setting sun. And he ran to the "Baleine," followed by Delphin and Fouasse, who darted forward tapping their backs with their heels and making the pebbles roll.

The "Baleine" was just putting out from the harbor when the news that they saw a cask out at sea was circulated in Coqueville. The children, the women, began to run. They shouted: "A cask! a cask!"

"Do you see it? The current is driving it toward Grandport."

"Ah, yes! on the left a cask! Come, quick!"

And Coqueville came; tumbled down from its rock; the children arrived head over heels, while the women picked up their skirts with both hands to descend quickly. Soon the entire village was on the beach as on the night before.

Margot showed herself for an instant, then she ran back at full speed to the house, where she wished to forestall her father, who was discussing an official process with the Emperor. At last La Queue appeared. He was livid; he said to the *garde champêtre*: "Hold your peace! It's Rouget who has sent you here to beguile me. Well, then, he shall not get it. You'll see!"

When he saw the "Baleine," three hundred metres out, making with all her oars toward the black dot, rocking in the distance, his fury redoubled. And he shoved Tupain and Brisemotte into the "Zephir," and he pulled out in turn, repeating: "No, they shall not have it; I'll die sooner!"

Then Coqueville had a fine spectacle; a mad race between the "Zephir" and the "Baleine." When the latter saw the first leave the harbor, she understood the danger, and shot off with all her speed. She may have been four hundred metres ahead; but the chances remained even, for the "Zephir" was otherwise light and swift; so excitement was at its height on the beach. The Mahés and the Floches had instinctively formed into two groups, following eagerly the vicissitudes of the struggle, each upholding its own boat. At first the "Baleine" kept her advantage, but as soon as the "Zephir" spread herself, they saw that she was gaining little by little. The "Baleine" made a supreme effort and succeeded for a few minutes in holding her distance. Then the "Zephir" once more gained upon the "Baleine," came up with her at extraordinary speed. From that moment on, it was evident that the two barks would meet in the neighborhood of the cask. Victory hung on a circumstance, on the slightest mishap.

"The 'Baleine'! The 'Baleine'!" cried the Mahés.

But they soon ceased shouting. When the "Baleine" was almost touching the cask, the "Zephir," by a bold maneuvre, managed to pass in front of her and throw the cask to the left, where La Queue harpooned it with a thrust of the boat-hook.

"The 'Zephir'! the 'Zephir'!" screamed the Floches.

And the Emperor, having spoken of foul play, big words were exchanged. Margot clapped her hands. The Abbé Radiguet came down with his breviary, made a profound remark which abruptly calmed the people, and then threw them into consternation.

"They will, perhaps, drink it all, these, too," he murmured with a melancholy air.

At sea, between the "Baleine" and the "Zephir," a violent quarrel broke out. Rouget called La Queue a thief, while the latter called Rouget a good-for-nothing. The men even took up their oars to beat each other down, and the adventure lacked little of turning into a naval combat. More than this, they engaged to meet on land, showing their fists and threatening to disembowel each other as soon as they found each other again.

"The rascal!" grumbled Rouget. "You know, that cask is bigger than the one of yesterday. It's yellow, this one—it ought to be great." Then in accents of despair: "Let's go and see the jambins; there may very possibly be lobsters in them."

And the "Baleine" went on heavily to the left, steering toward the point.

THE FÊTE AT COQUEVILLE

In the "Zephir," La Queue had to get in a passion in order to hold Tupain and Brisemotte from the cask. The boat-hook, in smashing a hoop, had made a leaking for the red liquid, which the two men tasted from the ends of their fingers, and which they found exquisite. One might easily drink a glass without its producing much effect. But La Queue would not have it. He caulked the cask and declared that the first who sucked it should have a talk with him. On land, they would see.

"Then," asked Tupain, sullenly, "are we going to draw out the jambins?"

"Yes, right away; there is no hurry!" replied La Queue.

He also gazed lovingly at the barrel. He felt his limbs melt with longing to go in at once and taste it. The fish bored him.

"Bah!" said he at the end of a silence. "Let's go back, for it's late. We will return to-morrow." And he was relaxing his fishing when he noticed another cask at his right, this one very small, and which stood on end, turning on itself like a top. That was the last straw for the nets and the jambins. No one even spoke of them any longer. The "Zephir" gave chase to the little barrel, which was caught very easily.

During this time a similar adventure overtook the "Baleine." After Rouget had already visited five jambins completely empty, Delphin, always on the watch, cried out that he saw something. But it did not have the appearance of a cask, it was too long.

"It's a beam," said Fouasse.

Rouget let fall his sixth jambin without drawing it out of the water. "Let's go and see, all the same," said he.

As they advanced, they thought they recognized at first a beam, a chest, the trunk of a tree. Then they gave a cry of joy.

It was a real cask, but a very queer cask, such as they had never seen before. One would have said a tube, bulging in the middle and closed at the two ends by a layer of plaster.

"Ah, that's comical!" cried Rouget, in rapture. "This one I want the Emperor to taste. Come, children, let's go in."

They all agreed not to touch it, and the "Baleine" returned to Coqueville at the same moment as the "Zephir," in its turn, anchored in the little harbor. Not one inquisitive had left the beach. Cries of joy greeted that unexpected catch of three casks. The gamins hurled their caps into the air, while the women had at once gone on the run to look for glasses. It was decided to taste the liquid on the spot. The wreckage belonged to the village. Not one protest arose. Only they formed into two groups, the Mahés surrounded Rouget, the Floches would not let go of La Queue.

"Emperor, the first glass for you!" cried Rouget. 'Tell us what it is."

The liquor was of a beautiful golden yellow. The *garde champêtre* raised his glass, looked at it, smelt it, then decided to drink.

"That comes from Holland," said he, after a long silence.

He did not give any other information. All the Mahés drank with deference. It was rather thick, and they stood surprised, for it tasted of flowers. The women found it very good. As for the men, they would have preferred less sugar. Nevertheless, at the bottom it ended by being strong at the third or fourth glass. The more they drank, the better they liked it. The men became jolly, the women grew funny.

But the Emperor, in spite of his recent quarrels with the Mayor, had gone to hang about the group of Floches.

The biggest cask gave out a dark-red liquor, while they drew from the smallest a liquid white as water from the rock; and it was this latter that was the stiffest, a regular pepper, something that skinned the tongue.

Not one of the Floches recognized it, neither the red nor the white.

There were, however, some wags there. It annoyed them to be regaling themselves without knowing over what.

"I say, Emperor, taste that for me!" said La Queue, thus taking the first step.

The Emperor, who had been waiting for the invitation, posed once more as connoisseur.

"As for the red," he said, "there is orange in that! And for the white," he declared, "that is excellent!"

They had to content themselves with these replies, for he shook his head with a knowing air,

THE FÊTE AT COQUEVILLE

with the happy look of a man who has given satisfaction to the world.

The Abbé Radiguet, alone, did not seem convinced. As for him, he had the names on the tip of his tongue; and to thoroughly reassure himself, he drank small glasses, one after the other, repeating: "Wait, wait, I know what it is. In a moment I will tell you."

In the mean while, little by little, merriment grew in the group of the Mahés and the group of the Floches. The latter, particularly, laughed very loud because they had mixed the liquors, a thing that excited them the more. For the rest, the one and the other of the groups kept apart. They did not offer each other of their casks, they simply cast sympathetic glances, seized with the unavowed desire to taste their neighbor's liquor, which might possibly be better. The inimical brothers, Tupain and Fouasse, were in close proximity all the evening without showing their fists. It was remarked, also, that Rouget and his wife drank from the same glass. As for Margot, she distributed the liquor among the Floches, and as she filled the glasses too full, and the liquor ran over her fingers, she kept sucking them continually, so well that, though obeying her father who forbade her to drink, she became as fuddled as a girl in vintage time. It was not unbecoming to her; on the contrary, she got rosy all over, her eyes were like candles.

The sun set, the evening was like the softness of springtime. Coqueville had finished the casks and did not dream of going home to dine. They found themselves too comfortable on the beach. When it was pitch night, Margot, sitting apart, felt some one blowing on her neck. It was Delphin, very gay, walking on all fours, prowling behind her like a wolf. She repressed a cry so as not to awaken her father, who would have sent Delphin a kick in the back.

"Go away, imbecile!" she murmured, half angry, half laughing; "you will get yourself caught!"

IV

The following day Coqueville, in rising, found the sun already high above the horizon. The air was softer still, a drowsy sea under a clear sky, one of those times of laziness when it is so good to do nothing. It was a Wednesday. Until breakfast time, Coqueville rested from the fête of the previous evening. Then they went down to the beach to see.

That Wednesday the fish, the Widow Dufeu, M. Mouchel, all were forgotten. La Queue and Rouget did not even speak of visiting their jambins. Toward three o'clock they sighted some casks. Four of them were dancing before the village. The

"Zephir" and the "Baleine" went in chase; but as there was enough for all, they disputed no longer. Each boat had its share. At six o'clock, after having swept all over the little gulf, Rouget and La Queue came in, each with three casks. And the fête began again. The women had brought down tables for convenience. They had brought benches as well; they set up two cafés in the open air, such as they had at Grandport. The Mahés were on the left; the Floches on the right, still separated by a bar of sand. Nevertheless, that evening the Emperor, who went from one group to the other, carried his glasses full, so as to give every one a taste of the six casks. At about nine o'clock they were much gayer than the night before. The next day Coqueville could never remember how it had gone to bed.

Thursday the "Zephir" and the "Baleine" caught but four casks, two each, but they were enormous. Friday the fishing was superb, undreamed of; there were seven casks, three for Rouget and four for La Queue. Coqueville was entering upon a golden age. They never did anything any more. The fishermen, working off the alcohol of the night before, slept till noon. Then they strolled down to the beach and interrogated the sea. Their sole anxi-

THE FÊTE AT COQUEVILLE

ety was to know what liquor the sea was going to bring them. They waited there for hours, their eyes strained; they raised shouts of joy when wreckage appeared.

The women and the children, from the tops of the rocks, pointed with sweeping gestures even to the least bunch of seaweed rolled in by the waves. And, at all hours, the "Zephir" and the "Baleine" stood ready to leave. They put out, they beat the gulf, they fished for casks, as they had fished for tun; disdaining now the tame mackerel who capered about in the sun, and the lazy sole rocked on the foam of the water. Coqueville watched the fishing, dying of laughter on the sands. Then in the evening they drank the catch.

That which enraptured Coqueville was that the casks did not cease. When there were no more, there were still more! The ship that had been lost must truly have had a pretty cargo aboard; and Coqueville became egoist and merry, joked over the wrecked ship, a regular wine-cellar, enough to intoxicate all the fish of the ocean. Added to that, never did they catch two casks alike; they were of all shapes, of all sizes, of all colors. Then, in every cask there was a different liquor. So the Emperor was plunged into profound reveries; he who had drunk everything, he could identify nothing any more. La Queue declared that never had he seen such a cargo. The Abbé Radiguet guessed it was an order from some savage king, wishing to set up his wine-cellar. Coqueville, rocked in mysterious intoxication, no longer tried to understand.

The ladies preferred the "creams"; they had cream of moka, of cacao, of mint, of vanilla. Marie Rouget drank one night so much anisette that she was sick.

Margot and the other young ladies tapped the curaçao, the bénédictine, the trappistine, the chartreuse. As to the cassis, it was reserved for the little children. Naturally the men rejoiced more when they caught cognacs, rums, gins, everything that burned the mouth. Then surprises produced themselves. A cask of raki of Chio, flavored with mastic, stupefied Coqueville, which thought that it had fallen on a cask of essence of turpentine. All the same they drank it, for they must lose nothing; but they talked about it for a long time. Arrack from Batavia, Swedish eau-de-vie with cumin, tuica calugaresca from Rumania, sliwowitz from Serbia, all equally overturned every idea that Coqueville had of what

THE FÊTE AT COQUEVILLE

one should endure. At heart they had a weakness for kummel and kirschwasser, for liqueurs as pale as water and stiff enough to kill a man.

Heavens! was it possible so many good things had been invented! At Coqueville they had known nothing but eau-de-vie; and, moreover, not every one at that. So their imaginations finished in exultation; they arrived at a state of veritable worship, in face of that inexhaustible variety, for that which intoxicates. Oh! to get drunk every night on something new, on something one does not even know the name of! It seemed like a fairy-tale, a rain, a fountain, that would spout extraordinary liquids, all the distilled alcohols, perfumed with all the flowers and all the fruits of creation.

So then, Friday evening, there were seven casks on the beach! Coqueville did not leave the beach. They lived there, thanks to the mildness of the season. Never in September had they enjoyed so fine a week. The fête had lasted since Monday, and there was no reason why it should not last forever if Providence should continue to send them casks; for the Abbé Radiguet saw therein the hand of Providence. All business was suspended; what use drudging when pleasure came to them in their sleep? They were all bourgeois, bourgeois who were drinking expensive liquors without having to pay anything at the café. With hands in pocket, Coqueville, basked in the sunshine waiting for the evening's spree. Moreover, it did not sober up; it enjoyed side by side the gaieties of kummel, of kirschwasser, of ratafia; in seven days they knew the wraths of gin, the tendernesses of curaçao, the laughter of cognac. And Coqueville remained as innocent as a new-born child, knowing nothing about anything, drinking with conviction that which the good Lord sent them.

It was on Friday that the Mahés and the Floches fraternized. They were very jolly that evening. Already, the evening before, distances had drawn nearer, the most intoxicated had trodden down the bar of sand which separated the two groups. There remained but one step to take. On the side of the Floches the four casks were emptying, while the Mahés were equally finishing their three little barrels; just three liqueurs which made the French flag; one blue, one white, and one red. The blue filled the Floches with jealousy, because a blue liqueur seemed to them something really supernatural. La Queue, grown good-natured now ever

THE FÊTE AT COQUEVILLE

since he had been drunk, advanced, a glass in his hand, feeling that he ought to take the first step as magistrate.

"See here, Rouget," he stuttered, "will you drink with me?"

"Willingly," replied Rouget, who was staggering under a feeling of tenderness.

And they fell upon each other's necks. Then they all wept, so great was their emotion. The Mahés and the Floches embraced, they who had been devouring one another for three centuries. The Abbé Radiguet, greatly touched, again spoke of the finger of God. They drank to each other in the three liqueurs, the blue, the white, and the red.

"Vive la France!" cried the Emperor.

The blue was worthless, the white of not much account, but the red was really a success. Then they tapped the casks of the Floches. Then they danced. As there was no band, some good-natured boys clapped their hands, whistling, which excited the girls. The fête became superb. The seven casks were placed in a row; each could choose that which he liked best. Those who had had enough stretched themselves out on the sands, where they slept for a while; and when they awoke they began again. Little by little the others spread the fun until they took up the whole beach. Right up to midnight they skipped in the open air. The sea had a soft sound, the stars shone in a deep sky, a sky of vast peace. It was the serenity of the infant ages enveloping the joy of a tribe of savages, intoxicated by their first cask of eau-de-vie.

Nevertheless, Coqueville went home to bed again. When there was nothing more left to drink, the Floches and the Mahés helped one another, carried one another, and ended by finding their beds again one way or another. On Saturday the fête lasted until nearly two o'clock in the morning. They had caught six casks, two of them enormous. Fouasse and Tupain almost fought. Tupain, who was wicked when drunk, talked of finishing his brother. But that quarrel disgusted every one, the Floches as well as the Mahés. Was it reasonable to keep on quarreling when the whole village was embracing? They forced the two brothers to drink together. They were sulky. The Emperor promised to watch them. Neither did the Rouget household get on well. When Marie had taken anisette she was prodigal in her attentions to Brisemotte, which

THE FÊTE AT COQUEVILLE

Rouget could not behold with a calm eye, especially since having become sensitive, he also wished to be loved. The Abbé Radiguet, full of forbearance, did well in preaching forgiveness of injuries; they feared an accident.

"Bah!" said La Queue; "all will arrange itself. If the fishing is good to-morrow, you will see—Your health!"

However, La Queue himself was not yet perfect. He still kept his eye on Delphin and leveled kicks at him whenever he saw him approach Margot. The Emperor was indignant, for there was no common sense in preventing two young people from laughing. But La Queue always swore to kill his daughter sooner than give her to "the little one." Moreover, Margot would not be willing.

"Isn't it so? You are too proud," he cried. "Never would you marry a ragamuffin!"

"Never, papa!" answered Margot. Saturday, Margot drank a great deal of sugary liqueur. No one had any idea of such sugar. As she was no longer on her guard, she soon found herself sitting close to the cask. She laughed, happy, in paradise; she saw stars, and it seemed to her that there was music within her, playing dance tunes. Then it was that Delphin slipped into the shadow of the casks. He took her hand; he asked: "Say, Margot, will you?"

She kept on smiling. Then she replied: "It is papa who will not."

"Oh! that's nothing," said the little one; "you know the old ones never will—provided you are willing, you." And he grew bold, he planted a kiss on her neck. She bridled; shivers ran along her shoulders. "Stop! You tickle me."

But she talked no more of giving him a slap. In the first place, she was not able to, for her hands were too weak. Then it seemed nice to her, those little kisses on the neck. It was like the liqueur that enervated her so deliciously. She ended by turning her head and extending her chin, just like a cat.

"There!" she stammered, "there under the ear that tickles me. Oh! that is nice!"

They had both forgotten La Queue. Fortunately the Emperor was on guard. He pointed them out to the Abbé.

"Look there, Curé, it would be better to marry them."

"Morals would gain thereby," declared the priest sententiously.

And he charged himself with the matter for the morrow. 'Twas he himself that would speak to La Queue. Meanwhile La Queue had drunk so much that the Emperor and the Curé were forced to carry him home. On the way they tried to reason with him on the subject of his daughter; but they could draw from him nothing but growls. Behind them, in the untroubled night, Delphin led Margot home.

The next day by four o'clock the "Zephir" and the "Baleine" had already caught seven casks. At six o'clock the "Zephir" caught two more. That made nine.

Then Coqueville feted Sunday. It was the seventh day that it had been drunk. And the fête was complete—a fête such as no one had ever seen, and which no one will ever see again. Speak of it in Lower Normandy, and they will tell you with laughter, "Ah! yes, the fête at Coqueville!"

V

In the mean while, since the Tuesday, M. Mouchel had been surprised at not seeing either Rouget or La Queue arrive at Grandport. What the devil could those fellows be doing? The sea was fine, the fishing ought to be splendid. Very possibly they wished to bring a whole load of soles and lobsters in all at once. And he was patient until the Wednesday.

Wednesday, M. Mouchel was angry. You must know that the Widow Dufeu was not a commodious person. She was a woman who in a flash came to high words. Although he was a handsome fel-

THE FÊTE AT COQUEVILLE

low, blond and powerful, he trembled before her, especially since he had dreams of marrying her, always with little attentions, free to subdue her with a slap if he ever became her master. Well, that Wednesday morning the Widow Dufeu stormed, complaining that the bundles were no longer forwarded, that the sea failed; and she accused him of running after the girls of the coast instead of busying himself with the whiting and the mackerel which ought to be yielding in abundance. M. Mouchel, vexed, fell back on Coqueville's singular breach of honor. For a moment surprise calmed the Widow Dufeu. What was Coqueville dreaming about? Never had it so conducted itself before. But she declared immediately that she had nothing to do with Coqueville; that it was M. Mouchel's business to look into matters, that she should take a partner if he allowed himself to be played with again by the fishermen. In a word, much disquieted, he sent Rouget and La Queue to the devil. Perhaps, after all, they would come to-morrow.

The next day, Thursday, neither the one nor the other appeared. Toward evening, M. Mouchel, desperate, climbed the rock to the left of Grandport, from which one could see in the distance Coqueville, with its yellow spot of beach. He gazed at it a long time. The village had a tranquil look in the sun, light smoke was rising from the chimneys; no doubt the women were preparing the soup. M. Mouchel was satisfied that Coqueville was still in its place, that a rock from the cliff had not crushed it, and he understood less and less. As he was about to descend again, he thought he could make out two black points on the gulf; the "Baleine" and the "Zephir." After that he went back to calm the Widow Dufeu. Coqueville was fishing. The night passed. Friday was here. Still nothing of Coqueville. M. Mouchel climbed to his rock more than ten times. He was beginning to lose his head; the Widow Dufeu behaved abominably to him, without his finding anything to reply. Coqueville was always there, in the sun, warming itself like a lazy lizard. Only, M. Mouchel saw no more smoke. The village seemed dead. Had they all died in their holes? On the beach, there was quite a movement, but that might be seaweed rocked by the tide. Saturday, still no one. The Widow Dufeu scolded no more; her eyes were fixed, her lips white. M. Mouchel passed two hours on the rock. A curiosity grew in him, a purely personal need of accounting to himself for the strange immobility of the village. The old walls sleeping beatifically in the sun ended by worrying him. His resolution was taken; he would set out that Monday very early in the morning and try to get down there near nine o'clock.

It was not a promenade to go to Coqueville. M. Mouchel preferred to follow the route by land, in that way he would come upon the village without their expecting him. A wagon carried him as far as Robineux, where he left it under a shed, for it would not have been prudent to risk it in the middle of the gorge. And he set off bravely, having to make nearly seven kilometers over the most abominable of roads. The route was otherwise of a wild beauty; it descended by continual turns between two enormous ledges of rock, so narrow in places that three men could not walk abreast. Farther on it skirted the precipices; the gorge opened abruptly; and one caught glimpses of the sea, of immense blue horizons. But M. Mouchel was not in a state of mind to admire the landscape. He swore as the pebbles rolled under his feet. It was the fault of Coqueville, he promised to shake up those do-nothings well. But, in the meantime, he was approaching. All at once, in the turning at the last rock, he saw the twenty houses of the village hanging to the flank of the cliff.

Nine o'clock struck. One would have believed it June, so blue and warm was the sky; a superb season, limpid air, gilded by the dust of the sun, refreshed by the good smell of the sea. M. Mouchel entered the only street of the village, where he came very often; and as he passed before Rouget's house, he went in. The house was empty. Then he cast his eye toward Fouasse's—Tupain's—Brisemotte's. Not a soul; all the doors open, and no one in the rooms. What did it mean? A light chill began to creep over his flesh. Then he thought of the authorities. Certainly, the Emperor would reassure him. But the Emperor's house was empty like the others. Even to the *garde champêtre*, there was failure! That village, silent and deserted, terrified him now. He ran to the Mayor's. There another surprise awaited him: the house was found in an abominable mess; they had not made the beds in three days; dirty dishes littered the place; chairs seemed to indicate a fight. His mind upset, dreaming of cataclysms, M. Mouchel determined to go on to the end, and he entered the church. No more curé than mayor. All the authorities, even religion itself had vanished. Coqueville abandoned, slept without a breath, without a dog, without a cat. Not even a fowl; the hens had taken themselves off. Nothing, a void, silence, a leaden sleep under the great blue sky.

Parbleu! It was no wonder that Coqueville brought no more fish! Coqueville had moved away. Coqueville was dead. He must notify the police. The mysterious catastrophe exalted M. Mouchel, when, with the idea of descending to the beach, he uttered a cry. In the midst of the sands, the whole population lay stretched. He thought of a general massacre. But the sonorous snores came to undeceive him. During the night of Sunday Coqueville had feasted so late that it had found itself in absolute inability to go home to bed. So it had slept on the sand, just where it had fallen, around the nine casks, completely empty.

Yes, all Coqueville was snoring there; I hear the children, the women, the old people, and the men. Not one was on his feet. There were some on their stomachs, there were some on their backs; others held themselves *en chien de fusils.** As one makes his bed

---

* Primed for the event.

so must one lie on it. And the fellows found themselves, happen what may, scattered in their drunkenness like a handful of leaves driven by the wind. The men had rolled over, heads lower than heels. It was a scene full of good-fellowship; a dormitory in the open air; honest family folk taking their ease; for where there is care, there is no pleasure.

It was just at the new moon. Coqueville, thinking it had blown out its candle, had abandoned itself to the darkness. Then the day dawned; and now the sun was flaming, a sun which fell perpendicularly on the sleepers, powerless to make them open their eyelids. They slept rudely, all their faces beaming with the fine innocence of drunkards. The hens at early morning must have strayed down to peck at the casks, for they were drunk; they, too, sleeping on the sands. There were also five cats and five dogs, their paws in the air, drunk from licking the glasses glistening with sugar.

For a moment M. Mouchel walked about among the sleepers, taking care not to step on any of them. He understood, for at Grandport they, too, had received casks from the wreck of the English ship. All his wrath left him. What a touching and moral spectacle!

Coqueville reconciled, the Mahés and the Floches sleeping together! With the last glass the deadliest enemies had embraced. Tupain and Fouasse lay there snoring, hand in hand, like brothers, incapable of coming to dispute a legacy. As to the Rouget household, it offered a still more amiable picture, Marie slept between Rouget and Brisemotte, as much as to say that henceforth they were to live thus, happy, all the three.

But one group especially exhibited a scene of family tenderness. It was Delphin and Margot; one on the neck of the other, they slept cheek to cheek, their lips still opened for a kiss. At their feet the Emperor, sleeping crosswise, guarded them. Above them La Queue snored like a father satisfied at having settled his daughter, while the Abbé Radiguet, fallen there like the others, with arms outspread, seemed to bless them. In her sleep Margot still extended her rosy muzzle like an amorous cat who loves to have one scratch her under the chin.

The fête ended with a marriage. And M. Mouchel himself later married the Widow Dufeu, whom he beat to a jelly. Speak of that in Lower Normandy, they will tell you with a laugh, "Ah! yes, the fête at Coqueville!"

Books published by Mondial

German Classics:

Heinrich Heine: Germany. A Winter Tale (Deutschland. Ein Wintermärchen. Bilingual Edition) ISBN 9781595690715

Johann Wolfgang von Goethe: The Sorrows of Young Werther ISBN 159569045X / 9781595690456

Theodor Storm: The Rider of the White Horse (The Dykemaster) German Classics. ISBN 9781595690746

Heinrich von Kleist: Michael Kohlhaas (A Tale from an Old Chronicle) German Classics. ISBN 9781595690760

Gottfried Keller: A Village Romeo and Juliet Swiss-German Classics. ISBN 9781595690791

Gottfried Keller: Ursula Swiss-German Classics. ISBN 9781595690838

Gottfried Keller: The Governor of Greifensee Swiss-German Classics. ISBN 9781595690845

Wilhelm Raabe: The Hunger Pastor German Classics. ISBN 9781595690753

Theodor Storm, Adelbert von Chamisso, Adalbert Stifter: Famous German Novellas of the 19th Century (Immensee. Peter Schlemihl. Brigitta) ISBN 159569014X / 9781595690142

French Classics:

1. Rougon-Macquart Series:

Emile Zola: The Fortune of the Rougons ISBN 1595690107 / 9781595690104

Emile Zola: The Fat and the Thin (The Belly of Paris) ISBN 1595690522 / 9781595690524

Emile Zola: Abbe Mouret's Transgression (The Sin of the Abbé Mouret)
ISBN 1595690506 / 9781595690500

Emile Zola: The Dream
ISBN 1595690492 / 9781595690494

Emile Zola: A Love Episode (A Page of Love)
ISBN 1595690271 / 9781595690272

Emile Zola: The Conquest of Plassans
ISBN 1595690484 / 9781595690487

Emile Zola: The Joy of Life (Zest for Life)
ISBN 1595690476 / ISBN 9781595690470

Emile Zola: Doctor Pascal
ISBN 1595690514 / 9781595690517

Emile Zola: His Excellency (His Excellency, Eugene Rougon)
ISBN 1595690557 / 9781595690555

Emile Zola: Money
ISBN 9781595690630

2. Other French Literature:

Emile Zola: Fruitfulness
ISBN 1595690182 / 9781595690180

Emile Zola: The Fête in Coqueville (aka The Coqueville Spree)
ISBN 9781595690869

Victor Hugo: The Man Who Laughs (By Order of the King)
ISBN 1595690131 / 9781595690135

Victor Hugo: History of a Crime
ISBN 1595690204 / 9781595690203

Honoré de Balzac: Ursula (Ursule Mirouet)
ISBN 1595690530 / 9781595690531

Honoré de Balzac: Maitre Cornelius
ISBN 1595690174 / 9781595690173

Anatole France: Penguin Island
ISBN 1595690298 / 9781595690296

Anatole France: The Crime of Sylvestre Bonnard.
ISBN 9781595690593

Gustave Flaubert: Salammbo (Salambo)
ISBN 1595690352 / 9781595690357

Romain Rolland: Pierre and Luce. ISBN 9781595690609

Jules Verne: An Antarctic Mystery (The Sphinx of the Ice Fields)
ISBN 1595690549 / 9781595690548

Andre Gide: Strait is the Gate (André Gide: La Portre étroite;
ISBN 9781595690623

André Gide: Prometheus Illbound. ISBN 9781595690807)

André Gide: Recollections of Oscar Wilde. ISBN 9781595690814

Other books:

Agatha Christie: Two Novels (The Mysterious Affair at Styles. The Secret Adversary.) ISBN 1595690417 / 9781595690418

Jack London: War of the Classes. Revolution. The Shrinkage of the Planet. ISBN 1595690409 / 9781595690401

Jack London: Before Adam. Children of the Frost.
ISBN 1595690395 / 9781595690395

Jack London: The Iron Heel
ISBN 1595690379 / 9781595690371

Oscar Wilde: The Critic as Artist. Upon the Importance of Doing Nothing and Discussing Everything. ISBN 9781595690821

Oscar Wilde, Anonymous: Teleny or The Reverse of the Medal (Gay erotic classic). ISBN 1595690360 / 9781595690364

Martin Andersen Nexo: Pelle the Conqueror (Complete Edition: Boyhood. Apprenticeship. The Great Struggle. Daybreak.) ISBN 159569028X / 9781595690289

Martin Andersen Nexo: Ditte Everywoman (Complete Edition: Girl Alive. Daughter of Man. Towards the Stars.) ISBN 9781595690333

Susan Coolidge: Clover. ISBN 1595690263 / 9781595690265

Jerome K. Jerome: Idle Thoughts of an Idle Fellow ISBN 1595690247 / 9781595690241

Malama Katulwende: Bitterness (An African Novel from Zambia) ISBN 159569031X / 9781595690319

Sigmund Freud: Dream Psychology (Psychoanalysis for Beginners) ISBN 1595690166 / 9781595690166

Getrude Stein: Three Lives (With an Introduction by Carl Van Vechten) ISBN 1595690425 / 9781595690425

Gabriele D'Annunzio: The Child of Pleasure. ISBN 9781595690581)

Frederick (Friedrich) Engels: Socialism: Utopian and Scientific (Appendix: The Mark; Preface: Karl Marx) ISBN 1595690468 / 9781595690463

Karl Marx: The Eighteenth Brumaire of Louis Bonaparte ISBN 1595690239 / 9781595690234

Carl Van Vechten: Firecrackers. ISBN 9781595690685

Bruce Kellner: Winter Ridge. ISBN 9781595690692

Printed in the United Kingdom by
Lightning Source UK Ltd., Milton Keynes
137018UK00001B/161/A